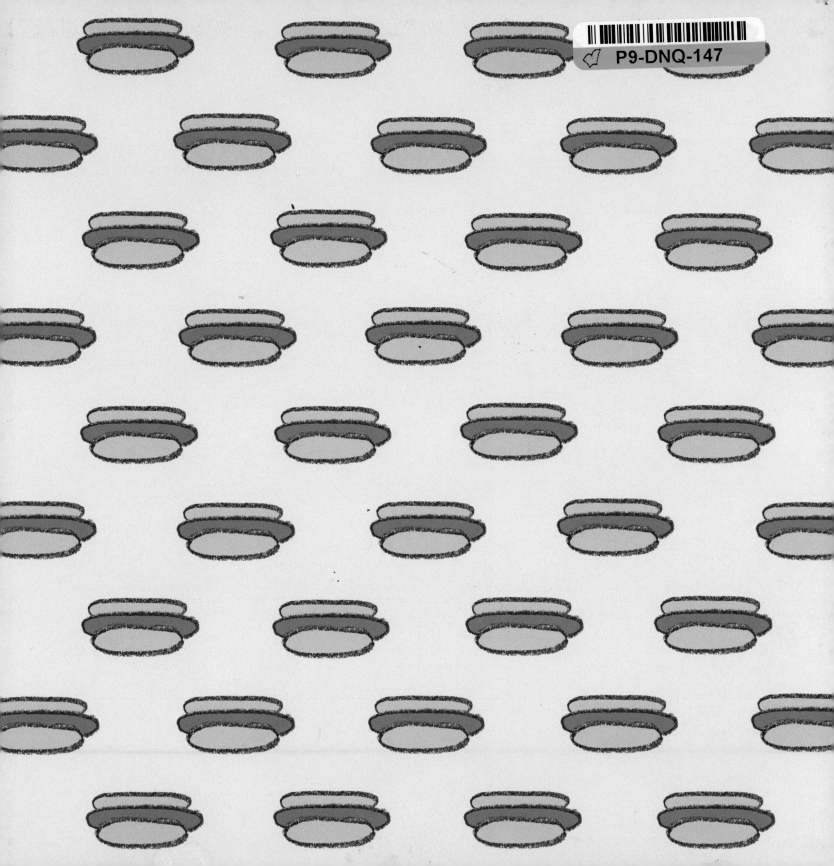

For Cheryl

Text and illustrations © 2004 by Mo Willems

First Edition, May 2004

Reinforced binding

This book is hand-lettered by Mo Willems, with additional text set in Helvetica Neue LT Pro and Latino Rumba/Monotype.

20 19

FAC-034274-18362

Printed in the United States of America

Library of Congress Cataloging-in-Publication Data on file.

ISBN: 0-7868-1869-7

Visit hyperionbooksforchildren.com and pigeonpresents.com

The Pigeon Finds a Hot Dog!

words and pictures by mo willems

HYPERION BOOKS FOR CHILDREN / New York
An Imprint of Disney Book Group

Is that a
"hot dog"?

I have a
question.

What do they taste like?

Of course!
Enjoy!

Go
ahead.

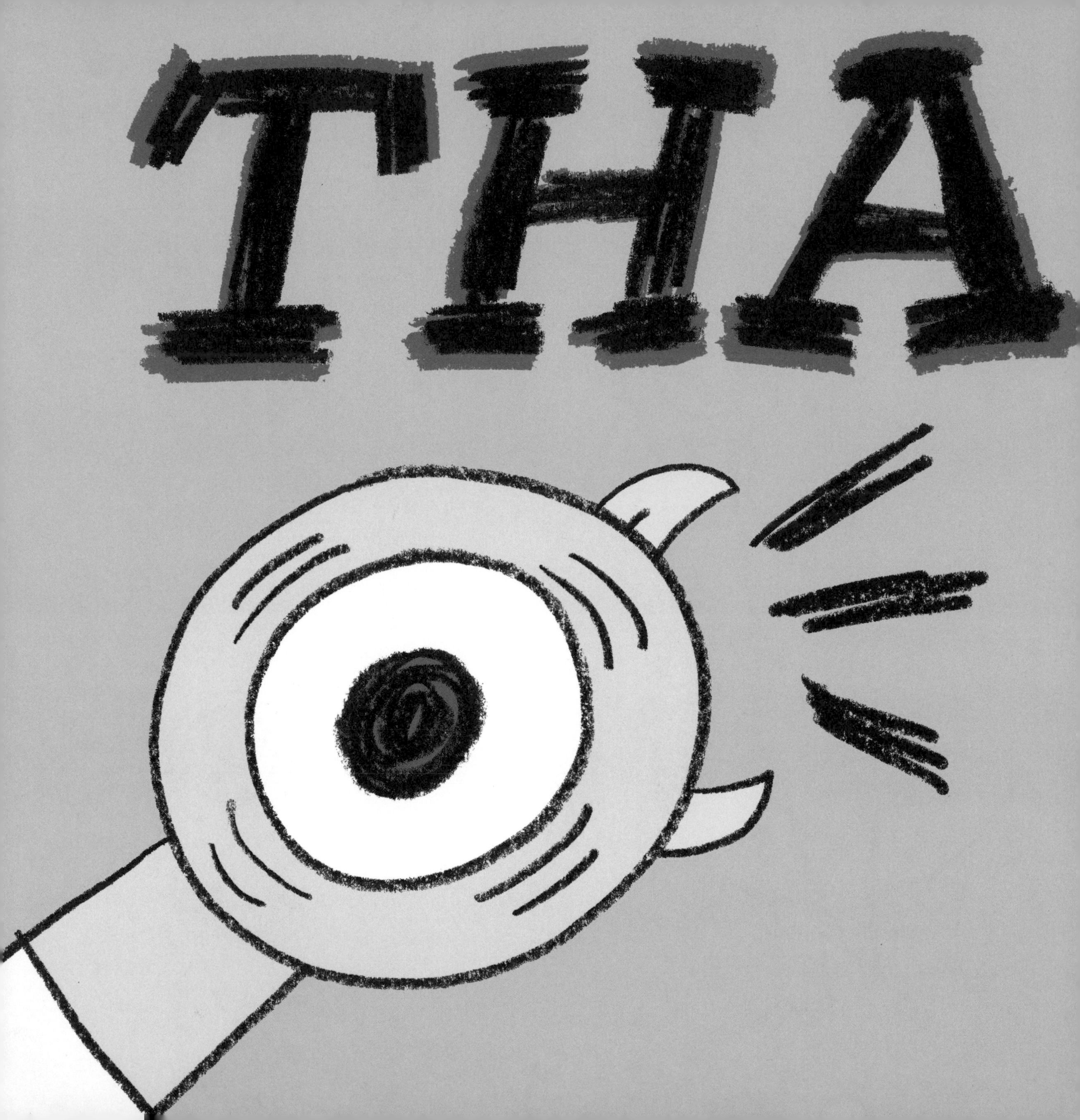
THA

T'S
IT!

You know, you're pretty smart for a duckling.